FITCH & CHIP

When Pigs Fly

Book #2

Story by Lisa Wheeler

Pictures by Frank Ansley

A Richard Jackson Book
Atheneum Books for Young Readers
New York London Toronto Sydney Singapore

Atheneum Books for Young Readers
An imprint of Simon & Schuster Children's Publishing Division
1230 Avenue of the Americas
New York, New York 10020
Text copyright © 2003 by Lisa Wheeler
Illustrations copyright © 2003 by Frank Ansley
All rights reserved, including the right of reproduction in whole
or in part in any form.
Book design by Abelardo Martínez
The text of this book is set in Palatino.
The illustrations are rendered in ink and watercolor.
Printed in the United States of America

2 4 6 8 10 9 7 5 3
Library of Congress Cataloging-in-Publication Data
Wheeler, Lisa, 1963–
When pigs fly / Lisa Wheeler ; illustrated by Frank Ansley.
p.   cm. — (Fitch & Chip ; 2)
"A Richard Jackson book."
Summary: Fitch and Chip learn that you do not have
to wear a cape to be a hero.
ISBN 978-0-689-84951-0
[1. Heroes—Fiction. 2. Schools—Fiction. 3. Pigs—Fiction.]
I. Ansley, Frank, ill. II. Title. III. Series: Wheeler, Lisa, 1963— .
Fitch & Chip ; v 2.
PZ7 .W5657 Wh 2003
[E]—dc21   2002013463
0114 LAK

This one's for my heroes:
Dori Chaconas, Stacy Dekeyser,
Kelly DiPucchio, Rhonda Gowler Greene,
Marsha Hayles, Shirley Neitzel,
and Hope Vestergaard
Love, L. W.

For Brennan, Sierra, and T. J.
—F. A.

Contents

1.

Knock. Knock. Knock.

Knock. Knock. Knock.

Chip knocked on Fitch's door.

Today was Hero Day at school!

Chip was dressed

as his favorite hero.

Knock. Knock. Knock.

"I am coming!" Fitch called.

Chip knocked loud . . .

Knock! Knock! Knock!

and hard . . .

Knock! Knock! Knock!

and fast.

Knockknockknockknock!

"I am coming!" Fitch called again.

Knock! Knock . . .

The door opened.

"Hello," said Fitch.

"I am ready for Hero Day.

Let's go!"

Chip looked at Fitch.

He looked at Fitch's

everyday T-shirt with the tree

on the front.

He looked at Fitch's
everyday brown pants.
Chip scratched his head.
"Who are you?" he asked.

2

Hyper Hog!

The two friends started walking
to school.

"Who are you?" Chip asked again.

"I am Fitch," said Fitch.

He hugged his tail.

"I am your friend from school.
Remember?"

"No, no, no," Chip said.

"I know you are Fitch.

Who are you dressed as?"

"I am dressed as my favorite hero,"

said Fitch.

"Hero?" said Chip.

He scratched his head again.

"You do not have a cape.

You do not have a mask.

You are not dressed like a hero.

I am dressed like a hero!"

Chip stretched his arms to the sky.

"Zoom! Z-Z-Zoom!" he called.

"Who are *you?*" Fitch asked.

"I am Hyper Hog, of course!"

said Chip.

"I do not know that hero,"

said Fitch.

"You do not know Hyper Hog?"

asked Chip.

"He's the brightest star in the sty!"

"I have never heard of him,"

said Fitch.

"He roots out evil!" said Chip.

"He must be a good hero,"

Fitch said.

He hugged his tail again.

"But I still have never heard of him."

Chip held out his cape and

zoomed around Fitch.

"*Zoom! Z-Z-Zoom!*

I never fail to save your tail!"

Chip sang out.

Fitch hugged his tail tighter.

"Hyper Hog is on TV," said Chip.

"I do not have a TV," Fitch said.

Chip stopped zooming.

He let his cape drop.

"No TV!" said Chip.

"Then you do not know

about real heroes."

Fitch stopped walking.

He let his tail droop.

"I *do* know about real heroes!"

he said.

"My hero is Timberwolf!"

3.

Timberwolf

"I do not know that hero," said Chip.

"What does he do?"

Fitch smiled.

"Timberwolf protects the trees,"

he said.

"He travels the world.

He saves the redwoods!

He saves the rain forest!"

Chip looked puzzled.

"Is he on TV?"

"No," Fitch said.

"He is in the newspaper.

Timberwolf is *real*.

He wears T-shirts and pants,

just like me."

Chip looked more puzzled.

"Can he fly?"

"Of course not," said Fitch.

"He is a wolf, not a bird."

Chip scratched his head again.

"Does he wear a cape?"

"No," said Fitch.

"A cape would get caught

 on branches."

"No cape?" said Chip.

"No flying?

 No TV?

I do not think you know

what a real hero is."

Fitch's ears twitched

the rest of the way to school.

4.

Heroes on the Playground

"Zoom! Z-Z-Zoom!" called a girl

on the playground.

She zoomed past Fitch and Chip.

"I will root out evil!"

yelled a small boy.

He zoomed between the two friends.

Fitch's ears twitched faster.

He hugged his tail tighter.

"Look at all these Hyper Hogs!"

he said.

"Yes," said Chip, frowning.

"Look at *all* these Hyper Hogs."

"I do not see another Timberwolf,"

said Fitch.

"No," said Chip, patting Fitch's

shoulder.

"Lucky you.

You are the *only* Timberwolf."

Fitch began to chew on his tail.

"It is okay to be the only Timberwolf,"

said Chip.

"I am always the lone wolf,"

said Fitch.

Chip scratched his head again.

"This mask makes my head itchy,"

he said.

"I have an idea."

Chip took off his cape.

He took off his mask.

He stuffed them both into his

backpack.

"That's better," Chip said.

Fitch looked at Chip.

Chip wore his everyday T-shirt.

He wore his everyday pants.

Chip did not look

like Hyper Hog now.

He was not dressed for Hero Day.

"I have an idea too," Fitch said.

He took out a green marker.

Chip smiled.

5.

Real Heroes

"Who are you guys?"

asked a small Hyper Hog

in a big mask.

Chip put his arm

around Fitch's shoulder.

"We are heroes."

"Yes," said Fitch.

He put his arm

around Chip's shoulder.

"We are *real* heroes."

"I do not think you know

what a real hero is,"

said the small Hyper Hog.

Then she zoomed around

Fitch and Chip.

Her mask was much too big.

"I never fail to save your tail!"

she sang.

She tripped over Fitch's tail . . .

. . . and fell into a shrub.

"Owie," the small Hyper Hog cried.

Chip helped her up.

He wiped off her knees.

He dried her eyes with her big mask.

Fitch helped the shrub.

He checked for broken branches.

He sang it a mending song:

"Branches short and branches small,

Branches grow up strong and tall."

"The shrub will be fine," said Fitch.

"She will be fine too," said Chip,

   patting the small girl's head.

"Is your tail okay?"

"I think so," said Fitch.

"It does not hurt much."

"Because you are a hero,"

   said the small Hyper Hog.

"And so is he!"

   She smiled at Chip.

"This pig is *my* hero!"

Then she zoomed across

the playground.

"Maybe we *are* real heroes,"
 said Chip.

"Maybe," Fitch said.

"But I wonder . . ."

"Wonder what?" asked Chip.

 Fitch scratched his head.

"I wonder what Timberwolf

would look like in a cape?"